The
Reading Specialist

LISA LEE HAIRSTON

ISBN: 978-1-4907-2903-9 (sc)
ISBN: 978-1-4907-2902-2 (e)

Trafford rev. 02/24/2014

 www.trafford.com

North America & international
toll-free: 1 888 232 4444 (USA & Canada)
fax: 812 355 4082

Contents

Foreword

> *But this book of the law shall not depart out of thy mouth but thou shalt meditate therein day and night that thou mayest observe to do according to all that is written therein. For then thou shalt make thy way prosperous and then thou shalt have good success (Joshua 1:8)*

Business Leaders maintain that anyone who reads and studies a particular topic one hour a day for one entire year, in the privacy of his or her own home, will become an expert in that field of study, regardless of whether or not he or she had/have a college degree.

If you spent that same amount of time reading anything your heart desired, what would you read? And after reading whatever struck your fancy, what or whom would you become after the readings?

Is it possible that you could land that one great career or that next great job irrespective of what is happening in the present-day economy? Is it possible that you could live in Infinite Abundance while others seem to suffer lack? Is it possible that you could create a whole new life for yourself in the least amount of time possible? And like the main character in the story, Prince Princeton Miles III, could you read your way back to perfect health?

I have written this book under the assumption that you are what you read on an ongoing basis. As you read this entertaining, but informative novel that is based on the powerful principles of Biblical Meditation (Joshua 1:8), may you become inspired to become your own *Reading Specialist* as you allow the gift of reading to take you places in your finances, health, relationships, marriage, career, and Spiritual Life that you have never experienced before.

It is true that no one will live forever, regardless of his or her present medical condition, sick or well, but is it not great to know that there is power in the Written and Spoken Word?

May you be continually blessed in knowing that you might be just one word away from the greatest adventure we call life!!! Who knows where reading will take you? Happy reading!!!

Chapter One

The Reading Agency

Miracle Faith Love loved to read. She was born to read. In fact, Miracle had often made the comment that "should she die, she wanted to be buried with a book, pen, and paper in case she woke up from death and needed to write something down." By the time Miracle had entered the 1st Grade, she was already reading beyond a 7th Grade level.

With such an amazing reading gift, especially at an early age, was it any wonder that Miracle would land one of the most coveted and prestigious positions with the Reading Agency? Just as a Temporary Job Service might go about finding the perfect candidate for a particular job assignment, Miracle was responsible for assigning the right reader with the right individual. Such an individual was better known by the Reading Agency as "our readee!"

Here is how the program worked at The Reading Agency. Each readee was a devout, avid reader, as was every member of the Reading Agency staff. Sometimes when the readee's schedule became too hectic for them to read for fun and pleasure, he or she would call the agency to send over a reader who would read the specified reading materials to them as they engaged in their regular work or routine.

For example, on one occasion, a male readee had an appointment with his physical therapist every Monday, Wednesday, and Friday from 2:30 to 3:30 p.m. During those rare moments, he needed a reader from The Reading Agency to read the stock market to him while he was on the table performing his regular exercises. No one seemed to mind the reader's presence during the actual physical therapy itself.

On other occasions, some of the readers would be sent on location to actors and actresses on the set who took time each day to silently read their scripts. In between shooting scenes, the readees might only have fifteen minutes to read their favorite books before getting back to work. Some of the actors and actresses were also infamous for having the readers sit next to them in the cafeteria and read to them out loud as they hurriedly devoured their meals.

On yet other occasions, some of the mothers who had just given birth to their new-born baby would call The Reading Agency in to read to their babies out loud while they, themselves caught up on much needed sleep and rest. In each case, the Readee would specify what materials they wanted to be read, and for how long.

The Reading Agency, as it was called, was founded by Princeton Miles III on October 13, 1980. Princeton possessed an insatiable thirst for reading books. Fortunately, Princeton was born into a royal family. His parents, King Princeton Miles II and Queen Margaret, had royal blood in their veins, and one, if not both of them was always running off into the sunset to handle some urgent business that usually lasted for months on end. How Princeton longed for normal parents to read bedtime stories to him each night before tucking him into bed.

Princeton was an only child and for the most part, Princeton had to entertain himself. Sometimes Princeton would get lost in one of the plots of his favorite books as he tried to figure out how the story would end. Other times, he would simply dress up in a costume and play act one of the scenes from a favorite movie. And yet at other times, Princeton would jump into bed and read out loud the whole book from cover to cover with exuberant feeling. These were those rare moments when his nanny would come in and take Princeton's book away and tuck him securely into bed. "Thank God for flashlights," thought Princeton.

Eventually, Princeton would grow up, and graduate from Military School with the highest honors. The day after graduation, Princeton left his hometown to go to the Air Force. He had never lost his love for reading, and it was through reading that he developed the passion for flying. That was the one thing he loved most when traveling occasionally with one or both of his parents—looking out the window to get a bird's eye view of what was below. "One day," he thought, "I will become a pilot and I can go anywhere in the world I want to go." The world is mine!!!"

True to his word, Princeton became a pilot. He was so good, he was offered a major position with many airline companies, but he turned them all down. His heart was with reading. He would now turn his attention to his education. The Air Force had provided him with many educational opportunities—opportunities that he made full use of.

By the time Princeton got out of the military, he was already set to pursue a Doctorate in Education. He had previously pursued a Bachelor's Degree in English, and a Master's in Education, with a concentration in Reading. Now that he looked back on it all, Princeton had no earthly idea how he had managed to squeeze in flight lessons and both a Bachelor's and a Master's all in what seemed to be one breath.

Princeton was in the process of planning his Dissertation Proposal, which he knew he would have to defend in the presence of the Dissertation committee. He was on course to write a Dissertation Proposal entitled: "A Love for Reading. Is it Nature Or Nurture?" Princeton had gotten this idea several weeks after opening the Reading Agency.

Initially, the Reading Agency started out similar to a Reading Lab. Anyone of any age, who was struggling with reading itself, or with reading comprehension, could come into the lab six days a week—Monday through Saturday to receive remedial assistance. Of course, everyone on staff was a Certified Reading Instructor.

After the Reading Lab had been in business for about a month or so, Princeton developed a Mission Statement for the Reading Facility, and upon doing so, the dynamics of Reading changed dramatically. The Mission Statement was based on the Bible Scripture taken from Revelation 1:3, which said, "Blessed is he that readeth, and they that hear the words of this prophecy, and keep those things which are written therein: for the time is at hand."

Princeton was so blown away by this Scripture in the King James Version the Bible, he compared it to the translation in the Amplified Bible to get a better understanding of what the Scripture was implying. It read thusly: "Blessed (happy, to be envied) is the man who reads aloud [in the assemblies] the word of this prophecy; and blessed (happy, to be envied) are those who hear [it read] and who keep themselves true to the things which are written in it [heeding them and laying them to heart], for the time [for them to be fulfilled] is near."

This very Scripture matched exactly Princeton's reading experiences as a boy, and throughout his whole life. He realized that there were many individuals who did not have access to a college degree of any degree, on any degree, but yet, reading books out loud was a passport to the world. Princeton was a prime example that books can take you anywhere you want to go in life. During one of his earlier experiences as an Academic Dean, he found himself in the perfect position to have access to every academic discipline the school had to offer.

Each Friday, Princeton would take one of the university's textbooks home to examine its contents and read each word from cover to cover—and that included the copyright date and information about the authors. One week, he would take home a Political Science Book. Another week, he would take home books on Public Policy,

Astronomy, Religion, and any information he could find on writing Dissertation Proposals.

At such a rate, he figured out that anyone who developed the habit of reading could become so self-educated, no one would ever know if he or she possessed a college degree—at least until an initial job interview, or if someone just got curious and asked. He wanted to pass that knowledge on to the public. It was his civic, moral, and spiritual duty—to educate the masses with books.

In any case, Princeton had many friends who also possessed a passion for books, reading, and learning, and they helped him to acquire books for his lab. Pretty soon, he had more books on hand than the Library of Congress, and that is the largest library in the world.

Princeton had to eventually move his Reading Lab to Princeton, New Jersey just to accommodate his infinite supply of books. Initially, he had set up his lab down in the south, near Atlanta, Georgia. But, he had to get back to his roots. His mom, Diana, better known as Countess Diana had been born and bred in Princeton, New Jersey and she adored the city so much, she named him Princeton so she would never forget her heritage and her pedigree.

The Miles' family came from good stock. They were in the top one-third of the income bracket, and they never let Princeton forget that fact. That is why his father insisted that he move near Princeton University upon his arrival home from the Air Force. They needed him at home to become the Prince they knew he was. Little Princeton would always be their Prince!!!

Chapter Two

The Reading Prognosis

Princeton Miles III was not going to take this medical diagnosis lying down, nor was he going to "just take it like a man!!! He was a Prince. His name was Princeton Miles III. He was a Veteran, for God's sake!!! He had the tenacity of the most determined, vicious bulldog.

In the Air Force, he had been trained to take excellent care of his health. He exercised regularly. He ran ten miles every morning—rain or shine. And he got regular checkups. This morning was no different as he reported for duty for his yearly physical. He had not been prepared for such a dim diagnosis.

According to the medical doctor, Princeton had stomach cancer, not to mention Type 2 Diabetes, and a serious heart condition that required him to need nitroglycerin tablets as needed. Being that Princeton's A1C was higher than 9.2% and his heart was beating more irregularly than usual, the doctor wanted to proceed as quickly as possible to prescribe immediate hospitalization and medication to expedite the healing process.

Princeton would hear none of that. Yes, he came in for expected checkups as required, though it had been years since he had retired from the military, but he did not have the heart to engage in any conventional or traditional medical treatments.

He had become an advocate, if you will, for non-conventional methods of healing such as alternative medicine, which he had read a lot about. In all the years of working at the Reading Agency, he had read just about everything there was to read on every subject, and he was most definitely not interested in traditional medicine, chemotherapy, or even heart surgery.

Princeton had read lots of information on topics such as meditation, yoga, genetics, acupuncture, hypnotherapy, and other forms of healing techniques, yet, when he had recalled the Scriptures he had read throughout his life, he did not remember if Jesus used any of these practices in his personal ministry while he was here on earth.

Would Christ condone such methods? Or were such methods he would need ahead of its time, and ahead of any theologist who might believe otherwise? Princeton would just have to wait and see. But he thought it best to rely solely upon the Word of God, with Christ as his Great Physician. After all, Christ is, and will always be the Great Physician. For the moment, The Reading Agency's annual Reading Summit was close at hand. He would certainly give this matter more serious thought.

Chapter Three

The Reading Summit

Reading for fun! Reading for pleasure! Reading for adventure! Reading for escape! Reading for relationships! Reading for entertainment! Reading for love! Reading for emotional intimacy! Reading for creation! Reading for travel! Reading for learning! Reading for information! Reading for wisdom! Reading for knowledge! Reading for revelation! Reading for career advancement! Reading for professions!

All these reasons for reading were the various reasons everyone from all around the world were ascending and descending upon the convention center in Anaheim, California. These were the very individuals who would stop at nothing to read anything and everything that was right in front of their eyes. When it came to reading, no reader would leave any stone unturned!

Some of these individuals were also the kind of reading lovers who would pay thousands, if not millions of dollars, just to spend an entire week uncovering the billionaires' secrets to wealth. These fascinating wealth fans were hoping to read any and all information at the Reading Summit concerning the top forty billionaires in the world, in the hopes of reading their way into that wealth status themselves. Yes, these individuals thought reading was absolutely priceless!!!

The Anaheim Convention Center was always booked more than a year in advance, therefore for this entire week, the entire center would be closed for business, except to accommodate the five thousand reading constituents who had already preregistered for the week-long reading summit.

Of course, Princeton Miles III was financially responsible for picking up the hefty tab. He had, after all, wanted to secure every square inch of the massive facility. One, being the royal prince that he was, "his highness" as some people called him, could afford to pay for anything his merry heart desired. Two, the Reading Summit itself had so many reading activities and reading programs going on simultaneously, with each room being virtually "standing room" only, Princeton had no choice but to book the convention center. Each ballroom was filled to capacity with its reading guests. Additionally, each room was also being utilized for some reading events not offered anywhere else in the world.

Some of the Reading Agency staff, for example, had their own reasons for attending the Reading Summit!!! Miracle was especially interested in spending the majority of the Reading Summit in the "Dissertation Rooms" where anyone who wanted to read the latest, published dissertations could not only read the dissertations out loud, but learn how to write one in the "Dissertation Lab" Seminar.

Miracle had always possessed a love for writing, and it was a life-long dream at the present moment to write an entire dissertation just for fun!!! She wanted to learn how to write a dissertation that would be an "A" paper, if submitted to an actual dissertation committee.

Miracle also wanted to spend a lot of time at the Reading Summit networking with any and every English Professor who might be either chairing or sitting in on the dissertation committee. Perhaps they could give her additional strategies for writing an effective Dissertation Proposal that could be easily defended to and by anyone anyone.

Lastly, Miracle had always possessed a passion to combine her love for reading with the prenatal world. She wanted to write a Dissertation Proposal on *The Effects of Deliberate Reading on Prenatal and Postnatal Development.* By "deliberate," Miracle meant that a parent could deliberately choose the reading material he or she wanted to read to the unborn child, in the same way that a concerned parent might censor the television programs or cartoons that his or her children might want to watch.

At the Reading Agency, everyone had a specialty area they gravitated to. Individuals, who loved finance would read everything concerning finances, including the stock market, and the latest information that those in the top 1% of the income bracket might want to know to increase their infinite wealth by way over 1,000,000%!!! Also, individuals who loved specific academic disciplines such as political science, history, accounting, or any other subject would isolate their reading exclusively to that discipline.

What if reading *Money* magazines to a child would predispose the unborn fetus to an affinity for acquiring massive wealth at an early age? In such cases, no one in the government would then have to worry about that person's financial well-being. And the child would not have to fret about the possibility of not having Social Security benefits when they reached retirement age. They would be financially independent, at any age after 65 or older!!!

Would a political scientist fare any better if he or she exposed their unborn child to political science readings? What would be the outcome of reading only political science material to the unborn fetus? What about other professions? Could they also use any reading materials to deliberately program their child with information geared toward that profession?

These were the questions that were on Miracle's mind during the entire Reading Summit. She needed this Reading Summit to provide her with those answers, or at least point her in the right direction. Her dissertation was counting on that knowledge, and so was the world, and anyone who would read her published dissertation, when that time came.

These same questions were weighing heavily on Princeton Miles III as well. He was here at the Reading Summit to literally *Read For His Health!!!* While others were Reading Money, Reading the Economy, Reading Wealth, Reading Prosperity, and etcetera, Princeton was only interested in reversing his negative medical diagnosis!!!

Princeton had read the Reading Summit's Itinerary a billion times. He had memorized every seminar and its room location by heart. After he opened the Reading Summit with an Invocation of Prayer and led the entire assembly into a collective, simultaneous, reading of Revelation 1:3 from the Amplified Bible, Princeton was going to head straight to the "Science Room" where he could have access to the world's most renowned medical doctors, immunologists, pathologists (those professionals who study diseases of the body), nutritionists, natural health practitioners, and alternative medical specialists.

He wanted to learn everything he could about his onset of cancer, diabetes, and heart condition so that he would be armed with the right arsenals to fight off every disease. He had no idea of what He would find, but, he, Princeton was open to any information. His health depended on it!!!

And everyone in the General Assembly had responded to the reading of Revelation 1:3 in a dynamic fashion: "Blessed (happy, to be envied) is the man who reads aloud [in the assemblies] the word of this prophecy; and blessed (happy, to be envied) are those who hear [it read] and who keep themselves true to the things which are written in it [heeding them and laying them to heart], for the time] for them to be fulfilled] is near." These words, which were the very center of the Reading Agency's Mission, were words that everyone lived by. It was their way of life!!! And soon, possibly the whole world would follow suit and make *Reading With Purpose* their daily routine!!! That is what the Reading Agency was all about!!!

Ultimately, this 2012 Reading Summit was an absolute success!!! All readers had gained access to the newest *Reading Releases* they were most interested in. Reading Lab Instructors had been taught how to develop more effective ways of making reading fun for their students as well as people of all ages and cultures. The Reading Lab itself had been equally effective in producing readers who had a desire to improve their reading fluency, articulation, pitch, tone, enunciation, pronunciation, and dramatics (reading with gusto and meaning) by 100%.

During one of the morning sessions, at least fifty of the top readers had one by one took center stage to take turns reading portions of the Book of Revelation out loud to the entire Reading Constituents during the General Assembly. Each person had read with so much passion and conviction, the whole auditorium burst out in uncontrollable applause after each reading. But, none of those individuals stood as tall as Miracle Faith Love. Something about Miracle's reading of Revelation 1:3 tugged at Princeton's heart!!!

Chapter Four

The Reading Audition

Back in Princeton, New Jersey, Princeton exuberantly tapped his fingers on his larger than life mahogany desk. He had just gotten off the phone with Chaplain Gabriel Marshall in Omaha, Nebraska.

The Chaplain had been his spiritual advisor in the Air Force. They had prayed together each time Princeton was scheduled to fly out on a mission. Before boarding the aircraft for the very first time, Chaplain Marshall had handed Princeton a small pocket sized Bible, with the special promise that Princeton would never take off for flight without having read the 91st Psalms. From that moment on, Princeton never went anywhere by sea, land, or air until he had read that Scripture. It was his "security blanket."

The Chaplain had not been able to attend the Reading Summit due to military debriefing, but he had been more than happy to fax Princeton the information he requested concerning healing ministries, healing crusades, and the nine gifts of the Spirit mentioned in 1 Corinthians 12.

During the Reading Summit, Princeton received a powerful revelation of how it would be possible for him to be healed of cancer, diabetes, and heart trouble. His healing would come through the reading of Healing Scriptures alone, and not through traditional medicine. That was the decision Princeton had come up with. And Miracle Faith Love would be the Facilitator of that healing!!!

As everyone on stage took part in reading portions of the Book of Revelation out loud, it suddenly dawned on Princeton that Miracle herself was a walking miracle, though he could not figure out why. He definitely knew by instinct—and he had excellent instincts—that there was something in Miracle's voice as she read each word with intense feelings and emotions—feelings and emotions he needed to explore in greater detail. Again, his life depended on it!!!

"Miss Houston, can you bring in Miracle Faith Love's file, please?" "Sure thing, Mr. Miles. Right away!!!" exclaimed Miss Houston. Princeton barely noticed Miss Houston's entrance into his office as she handed him Miracle's file. He had other things on his mind concerning what he would find in Miracle's career profile.

Miracle came to this organization seven years ago with outstanding credentials. Her academic training was impeccable. That was why he had not thought twice about hiring her on the spot. Miracle had received a Bachelor's Degree in English from Yale University, with a minor in Linguistics and Reading. Subsequently, she had pursued a Master's degree in Education, with a special emphasis in

Reading Curriculum Design. It was her desire to devise an Individual Reading Curriculum for each person who stepped into her immediate space.

Linguistically, Miracle had made the whole reading out loud experience at the end of the Reading Summit <u>Fun</u>!!! She had enunciated and articulated every syllable perfectly. Her voice was very pleasant and relaxing, but effectively penetrating. But, there was something more that was not just about the reading; that something was more abstract than concrete, yet spiritual. As Princeton hurriedly glanced over every single document in Miracle's folder, he found what he was looking for—in the "Tell Me About Yourself" section.

Miracle Faith Love had been a miracle child—a miracle baby. She had only weighed in at three pounds at birth. Her mom and dad, according to what Miracle wrote on her application, deemed Miracle's survival after birth a miracle. They believed, therefore, that Miracle had been born with the nine gifts of the Spirit mentioned in the Bible in 1 Corinthians 12.

They believed their Miracle had three of the Power Gifts: faith, the working of miracles, and the gifts of healing. This was how Miracle had gotten her first and middle name, Miracle Faith. The Love's also believed Miracle possessed three of the speaking gifts: prophecy, divers kinds of tongues, and the interpretation of tongues. Lastly, they believed Miracle had three of the revelation gifts: the word of wisdom, the word of knowledge, and discerning of spirits.

In His public ministry on earth, Jesus Himself possessed and walked daily in the nine Gifts of the Spirit, and Miracle was no exception. She, like Jesus, had at one time or another walked powerfully and dynamically in all nine gifts as well. On many such occasions, she seemed to zoom in and out of each gift at will, if not at God's Will, with little or no thought.

Prophetically, Princeton believed that Miracle's most prominent gifts at the moment were the three speaking gifts and the three power gifts. That was what Princeton was feeling as Miracle skillfully and powerfully read Revelation 1:3 out loud. Miracles would take place after she spoke!!!

When Miracle read, something on the inside of Princeton had responded to her "*verbal therapeutic touch*" through reading. Speaking of touch, Miracle had also written on her application that she possessed the ministry of the laying on of hands. She had that healing touch—a healing ministry beyond words. But, how would that ministry work for him to help him achieve Perfect Health? Miracle did not know it yet, but she was about to be auditioned for the Reading Audition of her life!!!

No one would be the wiser as to why they were being summoned to the "Reading Audition." All they knew is that Princeton had sent a memo to each Reading Agency staff member at the beginning of the week. The memo read as follows:

> *Enclosed in this memo, please find a myriad*
> *of Bible Scriptures that one of the Reading Agency's*

Readees wants read to them out loud from both the King James and Amplified Bibles.

Please familiarize yourself with these passages prior to coming to the Reading Audition on Friday, October 13 at 9 a.m. sharp!!! Upon your arrival at the Reading Agency, you will receive further instructions.

No Particular dress code is required, but please dress in whatever makes you feel most comfortable during your reading!!! Refreshments will be served following the auditions.

Additionally, My Army Chaplain will be on hand to monitor the Scripture Readings. Please do not forget your Bibles!!!

Respectfully,
Princeton Miles III

Some of the staff members immediately began reading the Scriptures out loud, just for practice. Miracle focused more on reading the required passages silently, first from the King James Version of the Bible:

"Surely He hath borne our griefs, and carried our sorrows; yet, we did esteem Him stricken, smitten of God and afflicted. But, He was wounded for our transgressions, he was bruised for our iniquities, the chastisement of our peace was upon Him; and with his stripes we are healed" (Isaiah 53:4-5).

"Who His own self bare our sins in His own body on the tree that we being dead to sins, should live unto righteousness: by whose stripes ye were healed" (1 Peter 2:24).

"And He said unto them, Go ye into all the world, and preach the Gospel to every creature. He that believeth and is baptized shall be saved, but he that believeth not shall be damned. And these signs shall follow them that believe; In my name shall they cast out devils; they shall speak with new tongues; they shall take up serpents; and if they drink any deadly thing, it shall not hurt them; they shall lay hands on the sick, and they shall recover. So then after the Lord had spoken unto them, He was received up into Heaven, and sat on the right hand of God. And they went forth, and preached everywhere, the Lord working with them, and confirming the word with signs following. Amen" (Mark 16:15-20).

"And when they had set them in the midst, they asked, By what power, or by what name, have ye done this . . . Now when they saw the boldness of Peter and John, and perceived that they were unlearned and ignorant men, they marveled and they took knowledge of them that they had been with Jesus. And beholding the man which was healed standing with them, they could say nothing against it. But when they had commanded them to go aside out of the council, they conferred among themselves, saying, what shall we do to these men? For that indeed a notable miracle hath been done by them is manifest to all them that dwell in Jerusalem, and we cannot deny it. But that it spread no further among the people, let us straitly threaten them that they speak henceforth to no man in this name. And they called them, and commanded them not to speak at all nor teach in the name of Jesus" (Acts 4:7,13-18).

"Wherefore, God also hath highly exalted Him, and given Him a name which is above every name; that at the name of Jesus every knee should bow, of things in earth, and things under the earth, and that every tongue should confess that Jesus Christ is Lord, to the Glory of God the Father" (Philippians 2:9-11).

"Christ has redeemed us from the curse of the law, being made a curse for us for it is written, cursed is everyone that hangeth on a tree, that the blessing of Abraham might come on the Gentiles through Jesus Christ, that we might receive the Promise of the Spirit through faith" (Galatians 3:13-14).

Here are the same verses in the Amplified Version of the Bible:

> "Surely He has borne our griefs (sicknesses, weaknesses, and distresses) and carried our sorrows and pains [of punishment], yet we [ignorantly] considered Him stricken, smitten, and afflicted by God [as if with leprosy]. But He was wounded for our transgressions, He was bruised for our guilt and iniquities; the chastisement [needful to obtain] peace and well-being for us was upon Him, and with the stripes [that wounded] Him we are healed and made whole" (Isaiah 53:4-5).

> "He personally bore our sins in his [own] body on the tree [as on an altar and offered Himself on it], that we might die (cease to exist) to sin and live to righteousness. By His wounds you have been healed" (1 Peter 2:24).

> "And He said to them, Go into all the world and preach and publish openly the Good News (the Gospel) to every creature [of the whole human race]. He who believes [who adheres to and trusts in and relies on the Gospel and Him whom it sets forth] and is baptized will be saved [from the penalty of eternal death]; but he who does not believe [who does not adhere to and trust in and rely on the Gospel and Him whom it sets forth]

will be condemned. And these attesting signs will accompany those who believe: in my name they will drive out demons, they will speak in new languages; they will pick up serpents, and [even] if they drink anything deadly, it will not hurt them; they will lay their hands on the sick, and will get well. So then the Lord Jesus, after He had spoken to them, was taken up into Heaven and He sat down at the right hand of god. And they went out and preached everywhere, while the Lord kept working with them and confirming the message by the attesting signs and miracles that closely accompanied [it]. Amen (So be it)" (Mark 16: 15-20).

"And they set the men in their midst and repeatedly demanded, by what authority did [such people as] you do this [healing]? By what means has this man been restored to health? Now when they saw the boldness and unfettered eloquence of Peter and John and perceived that they were unlearned and untrained in the schools [common men with no educational advantages], they marveled; and they recognized that they had been with Jesus. And since they saw the man who had been cured standing there beside them, they could not contradict the fact or say anything in opposition. But having ordered [the prisoners] to go aside out of the council [chamber], they conferred (debated) among themselves. Saying, what are we to do with these men? For that an extraordinary miracle has been performed by (through) them is plain to all the residents of Jerusalem, and we cannot deny it. But in order that it may not spread further among the people and the nation, let us warn and forbid them with a stern threat to speak anymore to anyone in this name (or about the person) [so] they summoned them and imperatively instructed them not to converse in any way or teach at all in or about the name of Jesus" (Acts 4:7, 13-18).

"Therefore [because He stooped so low] God has highly exalted Him and has freely bestowed on Him the name that is above every name, that in (at) the name of Jesus every knee should (must) bow, in heaven and on earth and under the earth, and every tongue [frankly and openly] confess and acknowledge that Jesus Christ is Lord, to the Glory of God the Father" (Philippians 2:9-11).

"Christ purchased our freedom [redeeming us] from the curse (doom) of the law [and its condemnation] by [Himself], becoming a curse for us, for it was written [in the Scriptures], cursed is everyone who hangs on a tree (is crucified); to the end that through [their receiving] Christ Jesus, the blessing [promised]

**to Abraham might come upon the Gentiles, so
that we through faith might [all] receive [the
realization of] the Promise of the [Holy]Spirit"
(Galatians 3:13-14).**

Tears welled up in Miracle's eyes after reading the
passages that Princeton had personally selected for the
Reading Auditions. She sat quietly for a minute or two,
soaking in the meaning of each word. Then she went to
read other translations from several other Bibles to give
herself additional revelation on the texts. When she got
home after work, she would sit down and read one of the
best Bible Commentaries on the market to get their point
of view on each Scripture. Miracle would be ready for the
Reading Auditions!!!

On the morning of the Auditions, Friday, October
13th, Miracle had dressed in her favorite purple dress, gold
jewelry and high-heeled gold shoes. She was the first to
arrive at The Reading Agency. Unlocking the door, Miracle
walked directly to the Agency's kitchen to prepare the
bagels and cream cheese platter Princeton had requested
for the Reading Auditions. She barely had time to pour
the orange juice into the pretty containers, and set out the
paper plates, cups, and napkins before the readings were
to begin. Someone else had been assigned to bring the
assortment of fruit.

Everyone had been instructed to sit in the Reading
Agency's Reception Area until he or she had been called
into the Reading Conference Room on the east wing of
the building. When Miracle's name was finally called,

she whispered a silent prayer, and walked briskly and confidently into the Reading Conference Room with her King James and Amplified Parallel Bible in hand.

"Ready anytime you are, Miss Love," said Chaplain Marshall. "Just take a couple of deep breaths and relax. Take all the time you need." Miracle cleared her throat, closed her eyes briefly, and then opened her tattered Bible of 7 years. It was obvious that Miracle had logged in a lot of hours reading the Scriptures. Even from where Chaplain Marshall and Princeton were sitting, they could easily see notes written in various colors in the margins of each page.

This Bible had been a gift from her dad, and Miracle had not had the heart to replace it with a new one. The words began to pour out of her like water. She got lost in the moment as she began to read the first couple of words.

It had not been her intent to just read the words as if she were a mannequin who could not move. She became the words, then she imparted them into Chaplain Marshall's and Princeton's Spirit!!! She never saw them nodding approvingly at each other. She did not think about how everyone else's reading went. Nor was she worried about the readers who were to come next.

She had been born to read!!! She had a Reading Gift that was second to none, and she would read with every emotion in her body until no emotion was left. She would pour herself out in rare form, as if she were reading directly to God Himself!!!

Trying to contain his excitement, Princeton calmly responded by saying, "Thank you, Miss Love. That was lovely. Please ask the next reader to come in, if you will be so kind." "Yes, thank you, Mr. Miles!!! Thank you, Chaplain Marshall. It was indeed a pleasure," replied Miracle. "You are quite welcome, Miss Love," said the Chaplain.

Chapter Five

The Reading Assignment

Princeton Miles III dearly loved Princeton, New Jersey, but with his parents' blessings, he was moving to Hawaii, and he would be living there for the next year, reading his way back to Perfect Health. And Miracle Faith Love would be accompanying him.

Miracle's reading had been spectacularly amazing. Princeton knew that her Reading Ability and Reading Gift was all he needed to reverse his doctor's medical diagnosis. But how would he convince Miracle to move to Hawaii with him? She had never expressed any desire to leave the Reading Agency, for any reason outside of her job assignments.

Should he or should he not tell Miracle about his health condition? He had deliberately kept his health a secret from the Reading Agency Staff, and from his parents, because he knew they would only worry. The last thing he needed was for their negative vibes to hinder his healing process.

Temporarily, Miracle would never know why she had been selected for this Reading Assignment. The less Miracle knew, the better. If Miracle was the bright girl he knew she was, with all those seen and unseen Spiritual talents, she might even figure it out on her own, even if it was only in part.

Moments after the Reading Summit adjourned and came to its conclusion, Princeton had flown by private jet from Princeton, New Jersey to Dallas, Texas to attend a major healing crusade. Chaplain Marshall had given Princeton the information on the healing crusade during the Reading Auditions.

Princeton elected not to fly the aircraft himself. Generally, he would be relaxed after such a solo flight, but he needed the extra time to think about how he would talk Miracle into flying half way around the world. She was a northeastern girl who had lived happily in upstate Maine before coming aboard at the Reading Agency. The only reason she had agreed to come to Princeton, New Jersey in the first place was to begin her Reading Career. It would take a miracle to convince Miracle to come with him to Hawaii—especially for a whole entire year!!!

Inside the Healing Crusade, the room was abuzz with chatter. Electricity filled the air. Princeton was happy he came to such an event. Princeton listened attentively to every health sermon, especially the ones that emphasized the words, **"I believe I receive my healing in Jesus' name!!!"** His faith for healing was soaring beyond the roof of the Superdome. Princeton just knew in his heart that he was healed—now!!!

During intermission, one of the healing crusade volunteers that he knew personally came up to Princeton to welcome him to the crusade. He gave Princeton some healing CD's, tapes, and DVD's. He would listen to them later once he got back to his hotel room tonight. In the wonderful atmosphere of the Hyatt Regency, he would find it easy to meditate while listening to those health tapes.

The Healing Crusade was well worth its weight in gold, and well worth the trip!!! He knew exactly what he would say to Miracle to persuade her to come to Hawaii with him to read him back to Perfect Health. He would merely tell her that he had gone to a healing crusade in Dallas, Texas, hand her all the tapes and ask her to listen to them. Then he would tell her that he would be taking off from work for the next year just for plenty of rest and relaxation. Her thinking that he was on a Sabbatical would work!!! Miracle knew how relaxed Princeton always became after his personal Daily Readings at the Reading Agency when he read out loud to himself!!!

Back home, Miracle looked at Princeton for a brief moment as if she were looking straight through him. Thinking about Hawaii and going there were two different things. Everything she loved and cherished was here in Princeton, New Jersey. To just pick up and go to Hawaii for a year was a stretch for her. "What would all her readees say," thought Miracle. She had grown very fond of each of them.

There was something in Princeton's eyes that made her accept this Reading Assignment. It seemed simple enough. All she had to do was move to Hawaii and read out loud to Princeton six days a week from 9 a.m. to 5 p.m. He had agreed to listen to his healing tapes after 5 p.m. and on Sunday's to fill in the gaps. He had no time to spare. His life was at stake!!!

It was also agreed that Miracle would live in the huge bungalow behind the mansion that Princeton would be living in. Miracle was young, single, and very much available, but she was an old-fashioned girl at heart who believed in the sanctity of marriage. She would never stay with any man she was not married to, for any reason. Thank God Princeton had understood. But from his perspective, he was just glad she had said, "Yes," to his Reading Assignment Proposal.

As they drove up to the large estate, Miracle took in the beautiful and lovely atmosphere. Princeton had been to Hawaii many times with his parents when he was a boy. He knew Hawaii like the back of his hand. As for Miracle, she had also come to Hawaii lots of times, during her "Reading For Pleasure" assignments assigned to her by The Reading Agency. Everyone always said Hawaii was the most beautiful place on earth!!! They were right!!! And this would be the perfect place for Princeton to get healed!!!

Princeton escorted Miracle to her new living quarters in the back of the estate. He cheerfully carried all her bags and luggage as she quickly assessed the huge bungalow. They were also near the beach. It was a gorgeous day and Miracle found herself getting lost in the rays of the warm sun beaming down on her soft, delicate skin.

Out of the blue, Miracle had a great idea that startled Princeton. She asked to see the mansion. She wanted to know as much about her new Reading Assignment as possible. Where would she be reading each day? Would she read in the same room each day, or would she have approval to read to Princeton anywhere inside his abode except his master bedroom and master suite?

Princeton had been temporarily caught off guard by such a question. He had had no idea that Miracle was this thorough. She was much more business-like and efficient than he realized. He loved this newly-found knowledge of Miracle. It had proven that his choice of readers for this Reading Assignment had been the right decision for him.

Miraculously, just being here in Hawaii was already working miracles for Princeton's health!!! He had no idea that he had been so tense, but being out in the Hawaiian sun, smelling the scent of the beautiful, greenish-blue ocean and white sandy beaches, the flowers, and taking in the beauty of the mansion's interior and exterior relaxed him immensely. He had no idea of what pleasant surprises the Readings would bring. But, if today was any indication of the things to come, Princeton knew his Perfect Health was on the horizon!!!

"If only his parents could see him now," thought Princeton. His parents, his mother especially, had not been too keen on the idea of his taking a year's Sabbatical to move to Hawaii. She had no earthly idea why he had made such a preposterous suggestion. He was royalty after all, and he had his duties to attend to within "the kingdom. They were never to know about his medical diagnosis or prognosis!!!

Chapter Six

The Reading Curriculum

Miracle's first order of business was to lie on her bed, close her eyes, and relax as she listened to the Perfect Health Tapes that Princeton was given during the Healing Crusades in Dallas, Texas. She would also study and re-study the DVD's to give her further Spiritual Insight and Revelation.

Miracle had no time to waste. She had sensed an urgency on Princeton's part, though she did not know what that exigency was. Miracle did not even take the time to unpack her bags or hang up her clothing so they would not wrinkle. She immediately got down to the business of reviewing and assessing the Perfect Health Tapes!!!

The first thing that came to Miracle's mind was Princeton's body language on the plane. Princeton had explained to her how he had always enjoyed flying over Hawaiian waters. He felt free, and uninhibited. He was beaming with joy as he stared into the blueness and the greenness of the never-ending ocean and white sandy beaches.

Princeton felt like he was five years old again, and that the world was his for the taking!!! That is how the ocean had always made him feel. And he was feeling like he could beat the cancer, diabetes, and heart condition Miracle Faith Love did not yet know about. He allowed himself to feel highly victorious in the matter. Defeat would never be an option for him. Defeat was not in his nature.

He was after all "A Miles!!!" For him, it was all or nothing. That was why Miracle was here in Hawaii with him. She would stop at nothing to be the world's greatest reader. At this moment, she was not just reading for anyone, any kind of way. She was reading for Princeton Miles III. As far as she was concerned, reading was her life, and she would for the next year at least, be at Princeton's beck and call. She would be the greatest reader he had ever seen!!!

Miracle was not a successful reader because she could read. After all, anyone could read!!! And she was not a successful reader because she had pursued and received a Doctorate in Reading. She read more than just books, dissertations, and reading materials during each Reading Session or for her Reading For Pleasure ventures.

Miracle read body language!!! She read faces!!! She read tones, voices, and pitches!!! She read the faces of the Readees and everything that was in the Reading Environment itself. She could read what people said, and even what they refused to say, or had no earthly idea of what was in their heart that they did not know how to say. She was an expert in reading between the lines and everything outside the lines. In her mind, anything and everything—person, place, and thing—were readable!!!

And she was reading Princeton's moods!!! Princeton was different here in Hawaii. He was happier. He seemed to have some kind of expectations about something. He looked like a bird that had just swallowed the canary. Whatever it was, she would maintain that happiness throughout every Reading Session with Princeton!!!

Princeton's happiness was Miracle's top priority for the year to come. And she would incorporate that happiness into every Reading. His happiness would be a part of Princeton's Reading Curriculum that she would meticulously design. She would see to it!!! But, unlike the Reading Auditions, Princeton had left it up to Miracle to design the Reading Curriculum. She would be responsible for deciding what she would read each day, when and how!!!

For starters, Miracle would begin each Reading Session by reading Revelation 1:3 from both the king James and Amplified Versions of the Bible. That was the central Mission Statement of The Reading Agency. Princeton had read that Scripture to everyone, every day at least a centillion times (1 with 303 zeroes behind it)!!!

Miracle believed that anyone who read anything at all from any portion of the Book of Revelation would receive an immediate blessing. For example, when she was at college, she had once taught a Bible Study on the Book of Revelation. She told everyone, "Read something from the Book of Revelation every day and you will get a special blessing."

Exactly twenty-four hours later, as she was walking to her Speech class, an older African-American woman came bursting out of one of the classroom buildings and began running towards her. Almost out of breath the woman said, "You do not recognize me do you? I was in class when you told all of us to read Revelation. I just wanted you to know I got my special blessing!!!"

When Miracle asked her what the special blessing was, the lady replied, "I was offered a job with a certain amount of pay. But when I actually got my check, the amount of pay had been doubled!!!!!!!" Miracle said, "Praise God, sister, and just keep on reading the Book of Revelation!!!!"

Miracle wrote down the following schedule in her Teacher's Planning Notebook:

9:00 A.M.-12:00 Noon: Read The Entire Book of Revelation from Chapter One to Chapter 22 three consecutive times.

Read the Six Healing Scriptures that were read at The Reading Auditions, in both the King James and Amplified Versions of the Bible 7 consecutive times.

End the Reading With Prayer.

12:00 Noon - 1:00 P.M.—Lunch

1:00-2:00: Read 20 Healing Scriptures in Both Versions

2:00-3:00: Begin Reading the Four Gospels, beginning with the Gospel of Matthew. Put special emphasis on the Healing Scriptures.

3:00-4:00 P.M.: Read Any Special Reading Materials that Princeton May Want To Read.

4:00-5:00 P.M.: Spend The Last Hour Confessing Healing Scriptures Out Loud, Especially Isaiah 53 and 1 Peter 2:24.

Reading Curriculum Subject To Change Daily Upon Request!!!

Miracle Faith Love was satisfied with the schedule she came up with, however, Princeton progressed so well, she considered the possibility of increasing the Reading Hours. Princeton's personal massage therapist came by the Hawaiian mansion, for example, each night after 5:00 p.m., and on Sunday afternoons to administer "therapeutic healing" through massage therapy. Princeton called such sessions, the "touch therapy."

The therapy was obviously working!!! Princeton was able to deeply relax in an instant and maintain that state of relaxation for longer and longer periods of time, which was a great facilitator of healing. Miracle thought it would be a miracle in itself if she could take advantage of Princeton's relaxed state of mind. Why, she could not figure out at the moment, but she just knew her additional Reading Curriculum Strategy would work even greater miracles for Princeton.

Miracle decided to begin her Reading the Scriptures every morning at 9 a.m. sharp, then break for one hour so that Princeton could schedule a 10 a.m. massage. She would either sit in the massage room with Princeton from

10 a.m. to 11a.m. reading the Healing Scriptures out loud, or she would go into a local Hawaiian store to purchase two baby monitors.

With the monitors, she would leave one in the massage room as she sat in another room reading the Scriptures out loud. At least that way, Princeton would have privacy during the massage session as well as have access to the Readings. If she stayed in the same room as Princeton during these deep tissue massages, she would sit in the room facing away from Princeton as she read aloud. Either way, whether she stayed in the room, or read in another location on the premises, neither of them—Miracle or Princeton—would compromise themselves sexually.

Princeton had preferred that Miracle stay in the massage room as the Scriptures were being read, but he knew Miracle better than she thought he did. He did not want to make her feel uncomfortable in any way. Nothing was to stand in the way of his total healing.

Princeton relaxed on the massage table as he listened to Miracle Read from the Bible. It was uncanny that even on the baby monitors, Miracle's voice was just as soothing, relaxing, and penetrating as it was in person, in the flesh. Now, he could focus on every Healing Word:

Bless the Lord, O my soul, and forget not all his benefits: Who forgiveth all thine iniquities; who healeth all thy diseases; who redeemeth thy life from destructions; who crowneth thee with lovingkindness and tender mercies (Psalms 103:2-4).

He sent His word, and healed them, and delivered them from their destructions (Psalms 107:20).

And ye shall serve the Lord your God, and He shall bless they water; and I will take sickness away from the midst of thee (Exodus 23:25).

That it might be fulfilled which was spoken by Esaias the prophet, saying, Himself took our infirmities, and bare our sicknesses (Matthew 8:17).

And said, If thou wilt diligently hearken to the voice of the Lord thy God, and wilt do that which is right in his sight, and wilt give ear to his commandments, and keep all his statutes, I will put none of these diseases upon thee, which I have brought upon the Egyptians: for I am the Lord that healeth thee (Exodus 15:26).

My son, attend to my words; incline thine ear unto my sayings. Let them not depart from thine eyes; keep them in the midst of thine heart. For they are life unto those that find them, and health to all their flesh (Proverbs 4:20-22)

Laughter doeth good like a medicine (Proverbs 17:22).

And the blood shall be to you for a token upon the houses where you are; and when I see the blood, I will pass over you, and the plague shall not be upon you to destroy you, when I smite the land of Egypt (Exodus 12:13).

And they overcame him by the blood of the Lamb, and by the word of their testimony, and they loved not their lives unto the death (Revelation 12:11).

The next day John seeth Jesus coming unto him, and saith, Behold the Lamb of God, which taketh away the sin of the world (John 1:29).

Beloved, I wish above all things that thou mayest prosper and be in health, even as thy soul prospereth (3 John 2).

And when He [Jesus] had called unto Him His twelve disciples, he gave them power against unclean spirits, to cast them out, and to heal all manner of sickness and all manner of disease (Matthew 10:1).

And when Jesus was entered into Capernaum, there came unto Him a centurian, beseeching Him, and saying, Lord my servant lieth at home sick of the palsy, grievously tormented. And Jesus saith unto him, I will come and heal him.

The centurian answered and said, Lord, I am not worthy that thou shouldest come under my roof: but speak the word only, and my servant shall be healed. For I am a man under authority, having soldiers under me: and I say unto this man, Go, and he goeth; and to another, Come, and he cometh; and to my servant, Do this, and he doeth it. When Jesus heard it, he marveled, and said to them that followed, Verily I say unto you, I have not found so great faith, no not in Israel . . . And Jesus said unto the centurian, Go thy way; and as thou hast believed, so be it done unto thee. And his servant was healed in the selfsame hour (Matthew 8: 5-10,12-13).

Therefore if any man be in Christ, he is as new creature: old things are passed away; behold, all things are become new (2 Corinthians 5:17).

But unto you that fear my name shall the Sun of Righteousness arise with healing in His wings; and ye shall go forth, and grow up as calves of the stall (Malachi 4:2).

For yet a little while, and the wicked shall not be; yea, thou shalt diligently consider his place, and it shall not be (Psalms 37:10).

I have seen the wicked in great power, and spreading himself like a green bay tree. Yet he

> **passed away, and lo, he was not; yea, I sought**
> **him, but he could not be found (Psalms**
> **37:35-36).**

By this point, Princeton Miles III was literally jumping out of his skin with great joy. Like the woman who felt in her body that she was healed of her plague, Princeton felt that he, too, was being healed of diabetes, cancer, and heart disease. He believed with every fiber of his being that when he went back to his medical doctor, he would receive a good report. He could imagine his doctor wanting to know how he had gotten healed in such a manner. He could also imagine that there were no traces of sickness anywhere in his blessed, healed body!!!

Up to this point, Princeton thought that his healing would be primarily through his Reading of the Scriptures and meditating on them. He had no earthly idea how positive the changes in his life would be. Each night as Princeton slipped into a deep, relaxed state of sleep, the words of health that he was getting down deep into his spirit and psyche, not to mention heart, were giving him additional clues that would help speed up and expedite permanent healing.

Princeton would have never guessed that he was the very reason he had contracted his sickness. He had no idea of how much toxin had accumulated in his body over the years. Princeton had eaten the best of food—after all, he was royalty, but he had never eaten organic foods. Plus, he was a constant complainer, surrounded by negative thinking individuals. He had gotten it from his mother.

As a result, he had developed a negative spirit. His negative countenance was probably the one contributing factor to his overall poor health. All that was about to change!!!

Miracle noticed subtle changes in Princeton that she could not explain. Princeton's whole demeanor changed dramatically one Sunday as they sat on the beach, out in the open sun. At first, she thought it had just been the transition from Princeton, New Jersey to Hawaii. Now, she realized that Princeton's mood had everything to do with the Scripture Readings and the sun.

Miracle had worked with many Readees who were often moody and depressed. In every case, their medical doctors had recommended that they get plenty of sun every day. Those who did were able to overcome momentary bouts of depression, none of which Miracle understood. She did not have a depressed bone in her body. Depression was just not in her genes. "But, if the sun was having this much of a positive effect on Princeton, perhaps he," thought Miracle, "would enjoy taking his regular doses of Readings outside in the open air, as he soaked up all that sun.

Miracle and Princeton sat on the beach during the early morning hours as he listened to her prophetic, magnetizing healing voice, which seemed to be therapeutic and magical. For the first time in his life, Princeton felt free as a bird. There were no unwanted demands on his time—time which he felt was invaluable. He looked upon his medical diagnosis as an opportunity to re-connect with his own life. This was the time for Princeton to become a man, and take charge of his own life.

He would spend this time in Hawaii redefining his life's goals and purpose. For what purpose was he put upon this earth—other than getting completely healed? He thought the military was his life. That was why he had stayed in as long as he did—for more than 25 years. The Air Force was not his life, as he had previously thought. "Nothing was wrong with a person's desire to serve one's country—especially a country he loved more than life." But, the military was only a part of it.

Who he really was in the deepest, innermost core of his being had nothing to do with the career path he had chosen. There was more to Princeton Miles III than met the eye, and he was determined to find that which had not yet come to surface.

His mother had never understood his need to be himself, which in his opinion did not have anything to do with being a royal. He would give up his throne in a heartbeat, if only he could get a moment of peace, quiet, and tranquility. What he was looking for was here in Hawaii—at least for right now!!! And perhaps that something had every—thing to do with Miracle Faith Love!!!

Chapter Seven

The Reading Revelation

Meanwhile, Miracle Faith Love had just broken down in tears for no reason at all, right in the middle of one of her Readings with Princeton. Even worse, there was nothing she could do as the tears flowed out of her like water contained within a dam. What was happening, Miracle had no idea. All she knew is that her unplanned response was due to the words that she had been reading out loud to Princeton.

One, it dawned on her that Princeton was here in Hawaii for a reason. She began to think about the possibility that Princeton's health depended on her Daily Readings, and that somehow, he needed her here by his side. What a burden to bear. Yet, at this precise moment, it was Miracle who needed Princeton—to just be there as she cried her heart out.

Miracle was highly religious and she had lots of faith in God, but she had no words to describe what she was feeling right now. She did not know that years of having to be strong emotionally and mentally as she took care of others had taken its toll on her. She was being healed emotionally and mentally. She was being delivered from years of inner pain, unnecessary worry, and bottled up hurt that she vowed never to share with anyone.

Had she not come here to Read to Princeton, perhaps she might never have made such an important discovery that, she too, needed an inner healing that most women just never talked about openly or publicly. "Perhaps," she thought, "That was the real, deep seated reason that she had always been fascinated by the mere thought of going into reading.

As long as she could remember, Miracle had always had a book in her hand. It was the miracle of reading that had kept her sane when all hell was breaking loose around her. Before today, the secret she bore in silence was only that—a secret she had not wanted revealed.

Miracle had been the victim of incest—beginning at the age of nine. She had been molested by her dad repeatedly until the day she chose to move out of her house at the age of twenty-one. No one knew that Miracle had been broken in so many pieces, she never thought she would or could be whole again.

Miracle's view of the world had been tainted and marred. She felt that everything she set her hand to was a failure. Never trusting anyone, especially those in authority, Miracle had turned to reading for consolation. Reading had become her friend—her anchor—her redemption—her Savior. As she read, she could go anywhere in the world, do anything, be anything, and have anything, without leaving her immediate space.

In Miracle's mind, everyone had an attitude. It was just so difficult to deal with people outside of her great Reading career. She had no idea that the person she most had to deal with was herself. Now, here she was, releasing years of emotions, in the presence of the one person she had admired the most.

Princeton Miles III had somehow been different with her. At some moments, she felt that he worshipped the ground she walked on. At other moments, he seemed to be the one person who understood her the most. He had treated her with respect and dignity, if she had any left, because it had been some time since she felt like she had any dignity at all.

Incest leaves a residue that never seems to wash itself off, no matter how hard you try. In Miracle's mind, incest must be the most horrific thing a young child can endure. The horror of surviving that one taboo that is too shameful to talk about to anyone is a miracle in itself.

Incest is that one thing that is yours alone to bear. No matter what transpires in your life, there is always that: "It is your fault" mentality. No one ever wants to own up to why the incest actually occurred. The abuser always tells you that "You are the reason you got hurt. If you tell anyone, they will never believe you!!!" And for the most part, no one does. They only look the other way. If you try to talk about any aspect of the abuse, no one really wants to hear.

Princeton Miles III had no idea of what was going on with Miracle at this moment, but he did the one thing that seemed to be the most instinctive: He just held Miracle in his arms until there were no tears left for her to shed. Princeton had no idea of how such an action on his part was needed.

Miracle felt safe in Princeton's arms. Like the woman in the Bible who let down her hair in the presence of Jesus, Miracle let her own hair down, not literally but figuratively. She let go of all the shame, the humiliation, the embarrassment, the resentment and the bitterness of not being heard by those who could have helped her the most. She allowed herself to heal.

Miracle did not believe in fate, but she did believe that coming to Hawaii to read all these healing Scriptures to Princeton out loud had had a healing effect on her that she had not anticipated. Had she literally read herself into much needed healing? Was Princeton himself trying to read his way into a healing that he was not telling her about? "What else was around the healing horizon," thought Miracle.

No one moved for hours. Princeton and Miracle both sat in the darkness "just being." The healing Scriptures had reached its intended target. Healing was taking place. And both Miracle and Princeton knew better than to mess with the power of all that healing.

No more Scriptures would be read for the rest of the night—by anyone!!! What had already been read was enough. Now it was time to bask in all that health and to soak in such a heavy healing atmosphere.

But, Princeton was too much of a perfect gentleman to remain in the mansion alone with Miracle. They were after all, not married. He knew Miracle needed comfort at that particular moment, but she would never jeopardize her high standards for anyone, for any reason.

That was when the Reading Revelation began to surface in both the minds of Miracle Faith Love and Princeton Miles III. Reading had been more therapeutic than Miracle and Princeton both realized, and they both had worked at The Reading Agency for quite some time.

As soon as Miracle could gather her composure once she stopped crying, Princeton would escort her back to her own living quarters behind the mansion to continue the healing process in her own way, under her own terms. It was Friday night after all and there would be no readings until Monday at 9:00 a.m. sharp.

Miracle finally settled into a peaceful night's sleep, if you could call it that, but not before wondering what she would say to Princeton early Monday Morning concerning her outburst of emotions. Next time, she would have to remind herself to maintain her composure and professionalism. But as for Princeton, she would just have to see what last night's revelation would bring.

Chapter Eight

The Reading Application

Princeton awoke at 5:00 a.m. sharp on Monday morning, as he had throughout his military career. He never started the day without a delightful cup of mocha latte and prayer. Today, however, something was quite different—Princeton Miles III was different. Rather than going into his massive kitchen to make his mocha latte, Princeton had a strong, unusual and urgent prompting to go straight to his prayer room!!!

Princeton knew that Miracle would arrive for work promptly at 9:00 a.m., but what should he do? He really felt the need to spend time alone in the presence of God, for the whole day. It was much too early to call Miracle to leave a message. Besides, after Friday, Princeton did not want to run the risk of alarming Miracle. She had been through enough already. He knew how hard it had been for her to open up to him about the incest. He had been the first person who had learned of her horrific secret when she finally broke the news to him once he had walked her to her door.

Princeton called what he and Miracle were about to do with respect to the Readings, his Plan of Action

(POA). He was about to take these Readings to a whole new dimension. And he would keep accurate notes of what happened as a result of saying "Thank you," millions, if not billions of times a day.

The Word of God, the Bible, was the Infallible Word of God!!!!!!!!!!!! Reading it was great, but without applying what has been read, one could not really expect to get from Point A to Point B. Not one time had Princeton said the words, "Thank you," since he had become ill. He should have been thankful that he had been diagnosed with cancer, diabetes, and heart condition in time enough to be healed.

Princeton should have been thankful that Miracle had said "Yes," to coming to Hawaii to read Healing Scriptures every day. There were so many things Princeton could think of to give thanks for. But, there was no time like the present to verbalize these words to God daily:

God Is Infinite!!!
God Is Awesome!!!
God Is Infallible!!!
God Is Incorruptible!!!
God Is Amazing!!!
God Is Magnificent!!!
God Is Marvelous!!!
God Is Great!!!
God Is Powerful!!!
God Is Almighty!!!
God Is Omnipotent!!!
God Is Omnipresent!!!

Now, Princeton hurriedly wrote down these words on paper so Miracle could begin incorporating these praises into her daily Reading Routine. Princeton would begin his day with Thanksgiving, Praise, and Worship—Today, and every day for the rest of his life!!! And Miracle would be a part of such a miraculous event.

Princeton soon discovered that the real miracle was not in his healing, but in his decision to make Thanksgiving, Praise, and Worship a daily routine. It had worked. Princeton felt better than he had at any other time in his life. Therefore, Princeton had gotten so caught up in the newly-adopted lifestyle of giving God Infinite Praise every day, He did not realize that the cancer, diabetes, and heart condition had gone—forever.

Princeton elected to unlock the front door and leave it slightly ajar so that Miracle would "see" herself into the living room, where they did their readings. He hoped she would understand that he was okay, but just needed alone time with God. He had never felt this way before— not even in the Air Force. Perhaps he would telephone Chaplain Marshall later this evening.

As Princeton stepped into his prayer room, he barely noticed his make shift altar, or the rest of the décor that he had painstakingly chosen to enhance his prayer life. For no apparent reason, Princeton burst out in overwhelming tears that he could not control, even if he tried. Perhaps he did not want to hold back whatever he was feeling right now.

Princeton, without realizing it, had gotten down on the floor to lay prostrate before his God. Suddenly out of his belly seemed to flow these words: "Thank you!!! Thank you

God!!! Thank you Father!!! Thank You Jesus!!! Thank you Holy Ghost!!! Thank you Holy Spirit!!! I give you praise!!! Praise The Lord!!! Hallelujah!!!" With each uttered word, Princeton found himself getting deeper and deeper into some form of Worship he had never entered into before.

"What was happening," thought Princeton. Many times, Miracle had read the Book of Revelation and the Book of Psalms. He had listened attentively to every word, as he had with every word that Miracle read to him. All the Scriptures that Miracle had read to him from the Psalms were coming into his psyche.

> **"Enter into His gates with thanksgiving and into His courts with praise. Be thankful unto Him and bless His name. For the Lord is good, His mercy is everlasting, and his truth endureth to all generations" (Psalms 100:4). "O Lord, our Lord, how excellent is thy name in all the earth" (Psalms 8:1). "From the rising of the sun until the going down of the same, the Lord's name is to be praised" (Psalms 113:3). Seven times a day do I Praise thee because of thy righteous judgments" (Psalms 119:164).**

And Princeton had paid close attention to Miracle's reading from the Book of Revelation, specifically from Revelation 5:11-14: "And I beheld, and I heard the voice of many angels round about the throne and the beasts and the elders: and the number of them was ten thousand times ten thousand, and thousands of thousands; saying with a loud voice, Worthy is the Lamb that was slain to receive power, and riches, and wisdom, and strength, and honour, and glory, and blessing.

And every creature which is in Heaven, and on the earth, and under the earth, and such as are in the sea, and all that are in them, heard I saying, Blessing, and honour, and Glory, and power, be until him that sitteth upon the throne, and unto the Lamb forever and ever. And the four beasts said, Amen. And the four and twenty elders fell down and worshipped Him that liveth forever and ever."

Was this what was happening to Princeton? He felt like he was standing in the throne room of God, in His very presence, just waiting to Worship Him and do His bidding like the angels. Was this what Jesus meant when He said in the Lord's Prayer, "Thy will be done on earth, as it is in Heaven" (Matthew 6:10)? If it were, Princeton wanted in!!!

Presently, Miracle also wanted in—into Princeton's living room. She did not understand what was wrong. She had rang the doorbell three times. Where was Princeton? Why did he have the door slightly open? Should she go in? Should she call out to Princeton? It was 9:00 a.m. sharp. Princeton woke up every day at 5 a.m. just like clockwork. He must have unlocked the door on purpose. After all, Princeton had never left the door unlocked before.

Entering into the living room, there was no sign of Princeton. She was not accustomed to walking around in the mansion, even when Princeton was present. She felt like an intruder at this point, but she forced herself to walk down the mansion's corridor. Out of the blue, Miracle heard Princeton speaking, but to whom? No one else was here.

Miracle was relieved to know Princeton was okay. Perhaps he was on the phone with the Chaplain. As Miracle approached the room where Princeton seemed to be, she was shocked to see him lying on the floor in tears. Was she having a flashback of Friday night? Was she having a déjà vu moment? Miracle stood still, watching Princeton for a few more seconds before moving. Then, it dawned on her that Princeton was praying in a manner she had never seen him pray before.

Princeton was also shouting at the top of his lungs, with gusto, all the Bible Scriptures on Healing that she, herself, had been privileged to read to him during the Readings.

Princeton begun everyone's day at the Reading Agency with prayer before they began their Reading Routine, but Princeton was in rare form today. Not wanting to disturb Princeton, or spoil the moment, Miracle turned to walk back into the living room, and just wait. That was when Princeton stood up abruptly. He had sensed her presence.

"O, there you are, Miracle. I knew you would be here at 9:00 on the dot, but, surprisingly, I have been in some form of Praise and Worship for four hours. I have not even had my morning latte yet. At this point, I do not even feel like moving. All I can do right now is just say, "Thank you God. Thank you God, etcetera.

I hope you do not mind if I cancel today's reading. I am just not up to reading anything right now. Would you be a dear and go Online and download a document I once read on the multiple ways you can say the word, "Thank you!!!" in over 400 languages. You are free to use my office if you like. Tomorrow morning at the same usual time, I want you to read the list to me. Together, we will work through any pronunciation issues that we might have."

Up to now, for the last six months, the Readings on Healing Scriptures have been great, but now I want you to focus your readings specifically on Thanksgiving, Praise, and Worship. Do not ask me why: I do not even know why myself yet, but I must go with what my heart is saying to me right now."

I must get back to whatever I was feeling back in my prayer room. I hope you will understand. Just see yourself out when you leave, and make sure the front door is locked before you go. I look forward to seeing you tomorrow!!!

Miracle took up Princeton's offer to download his necessary information on his computer. It took her a couple of hours to find the list that Princeton was hoping to acquire for the reading. She had no idea that there were so many ways one could say, "Thank you." She herself was a reader, and she considered herself to be somewhat of a linguist, but not one time had she thought about saying, "Thank you," in English, let alone in French, Spanish or any other language.

"Merci beaucoup, (French)" "Muchos Gracias, (Spanish) and "Grazie." (Italian). Saying these words out loud sent cold chills up Miracle's spine!!! What would God think if she herself were to say, "Thank you," in any language? She was anxious to get started with saying the words herself. She would see where saying, "Thank you" would lead.

Chapter Nine

The Reading Results

The medical doctor could not explain why Princeton Miles III was completely healed of diabetes, stomach cancer, and a serious, life-threatening heart disease. Princeton had refused all forms of conventional, traditional, and recommended medical treatments known to man, opting instead to throw himself upon the mercy of God and having Healing Scriptures Read to him Daily. He had considered alternative medicine but realized that "with His Stripes we are healed."

Christ was His Healer, and Princeton wanted the world at large to know that The Word of God is the Final Authority on Healing. He would look to the Word and only to the word for his healing. As far as Princeton was concerned, God would have the final say concerning every aspect of his "long life" mentioned in Psalms 91.

This time last year, Princeton's diagnosis had been 100% accurate. At best, Princeton had no less than three months to live. Princeton had been told to go home and get his house in order and to make the most of his remaining days on the earth. No one in the field of medical science had the technology, know how, or intellect to pull out a miracle for their beloved Prince.

Now, this medical doctor could only do what seemed the most logical thing to do. He sent Princeton on a wild goose chase by arranging for a host of medical specialists to re-evaluate Princeton's health. These were the specialists that were at the top of their game medically. They were the best medical science had to offer.

One by one, each medical doctor and specialist had to concede that there was no medical explanation as to how Princeton now stood before them as a picture and epitome of Perfect Health. Princeton did not have one single iota of sickness anywhere in his now Perfectly Healthy body.

Everyone, from the stomach specialist to the mental health practitioners, concurred that this sickness to health story was the greatest phenomenon they had ever encountered!!! A battery of tests was being set up for further research study at the highest level known to mankind. The doctor had even joked that Princeton must have a twin brother somewhere, because he had never seen anyone heal so quickly, especially without the intervention of traditional forms of medical treatment.

For Princeton, there had been no chemo, no medication, no loss of hair, and other cancer symptoms patients experienced during their illness. But, was it the readings, the moving to Hawaii, music therapy (listening to Gospel songs on CD), massage therapy, relaxation techniques, forgiveness techniques (saying "I Forgive You" Millions of times a day), or the Thanksgiving, Praise, and

Worship, that worked? Or was it a combination of these methodologies, or was it just the readings, or just one of the other components? No one really knew.

Princeton was healed—academically, emotionally, financially, mentally, physically, socially, and spiritually. It was as if he had gone back into his life, beginning in his mother's womb, and had been birthed and reborn, grown up, and healed every single aspect of his life. He had healed every hurt, and every wound by forgiving the past and letting it go. He would be okay, and so would Miracle.

The medical doctors were trying to intellectualize what Princeton had known for months—that there was a God in Heaven who still specialized in miracles—his miracle being none other than Miracle Faith Love in the flesh!!!

With respect to Princeton's heart, he had had no earthly idea just how badly his heart needed a heart transplant or by-pass surgery as the doctors had recommended one year ago today!!! Such a dismal and drab prognosis was just the outward indication of a heart issue that was deeply rooted within himself.

The Bible says to "Keep thy heart for "out of it springs the issues of life" (Proverbs 4:23). And Princeton had an issue with his past, his childhood, and his role as a prince and future king. The issue for Princeton had started with his parents, namely his domineering mother. The throne and the whole concept of being a queen and keeping up "royal appearances" were everything to his mother.

For that reason alone, Princeton had missed out on having his parents, the king and queen, read bedtime stories to him each night before tucking him into bed. The king and queen had always been too busy galloping about the globe engaged in some royal duty. The king and queen had been highly popular with the people they ruled; this popularity had meant nothing to Princeton.

Princeton just needed his mom and dad. "A hug every now and then would have also sufficed immensely," thought Princeton. But affection was not the king or queen's cup of tea. They thought more about the constituents they ruled and governed than they thought of him.

Princeton had no idea that such a feeling of bitterness and anger was affecting his heart so much. Is it any wonder that he felt like he needed a brand new heart!!! Princeton's heart was literally torn apart by a lack of love he desperately needed from the parents he loved more than life itself.

If only his father had had a backbone and stood up to his wife, the queen. If only his dad, the king, had asserted his position on the throne and overruled the queen. Princeton viewed his own dad as being too weak to stand up to his own wife.

To make matters worse, both his mom and dad were putting too much pressure on him to step into their shoes one day as the new king. They were breeding him to sit on the throne. All Princeton wanted and needed was a normal life. He had no desire to be a prince, let alone a king, or <u>the</u> king. He just wanted normalcy.

All these specialists, as well-meaning as they were, had no idea that Princeton only needed two specialists in his life right now—God, his very own Creator, and Miracle Faith Love—*The Reading Specialist!!!*

Every day for the past year, Miracle had read Bible Scriptures and other Readings Princeton himself had deliberately prescribed and arranged. That would be his miracle. Christ is the Great Physician and the Wonderful Counselor who has never lost a case, and Miracle Faith Love was just what the Great Physician, Christ, had ordered!!!

Miracle had literally read Princeton back to life and Perfect Health when the medical doctors had one of his feet in the grave already. All the Healing Scriptures had worked!!! Why? One, God was Omnipotent and Omnipresent, not to mention absolutely Sovereign!!!

Two, both Princeton and Miracle Faith Love worked at the Reading Agency with a slew of other Reading staff. No one, not even Princeton, really viewed himself as the Reading Agency's president and founder. They all were Reading Specialists who specialized in Reading whatever the readee needed read, for whatever reason.

The whole Reading staff were well adept at reading to anyone of any age, from the prenatal stage when the embryo and/or fetus was still resting comfortably in his or her mother's precious womb, to the senior citizens in nursing homes anywhere in the world.

Princeton had been smart enough to hire Miracle to read to him while in Hawaii for one year, though she had never known why she was doing so. At some point, Princeton had gathered that Miracle had somehow been bright enough to figure out why she was here in Hawaii. Perhaps he had read it in her eyes that she suspected something was out of the ordinary as to the real reason they both found themselves here in Hawaii.

He could not worry about that for right now. Princeton had isolated his three medical conditions into three separate and distinct Readings—Readings for the stomach cancer, Readings for the diabetes, and Readings for his heart condition, and in all scenarios, Miracle would be here for him—whether she knew of his medical condition or not.

Princeton's heart was healed because he had asked Miracle to read out loud to him every Scripture in the Bible that had the word, "heart" in it. For example:

- **Keep thy heart with all diligence, for out of it are the issues of life (Proverbs 4:23).**
- **Blessed are the pure in heart, for they shall see God (Matthew 5:8)**
- **Let not your heart be troubled. Ye believe in God, believe also in me (John 14).**
- **But those things which proceed out of the mouth come forth from the heart; and they defile the man. For out of the heart proceed evil thoughts, murders, adulteries, fornications, thefts, false witness, blasphemies; these are the things which defile a man, but to eat with unwashen hands defileth not a man (Matthew 15:18-20).**
- **A merry heart doeth good like a medicine (Proverbs 17:22).**

Princeton had goals concerning his desire for a new heart without medication or surgery. One, "**Cast away from you all your transgressions, whereby, ye have transgressed and make you a new heart and a new spirit . . . For I have no pleasure in him that dieth . . ."** (Ezekiel 18:31,32)

Two, **a new heart also will I give you, and a new spirit will I put within you, and I will take away the stony heart out of your flesh, and I will give you a heart of flesh"** (Ezekiel 36:26).

Three, **praise ye the Lord. Blessed is the man that feareth the Lord that delighteth greatly in His commandments. His seed shall be mighty upon earth; the upright shall be blessed. Wealth and riches shall be in his house; and his righteousness endureth forever. Unto the upright there ariseth light in the darkness; he is gracious, and full of compassion and righteous. A good man sheweth favour and lendeth, he will guide his affairs with discretion. Surely he will not be moved forever, the righteous shall be in everlasting remembrance. He shall not be afraid of evid tidings, his heart is fixed, trusting in the Lord. His heart is established, he shall not be afraid until he see his desire upon his enemies"** (Psalms 112).

He hath dispersed, he hath given to the poor; his righteousness endureth forever, his horn shall be exalted with honour. The wicked shall see it, and be grieved. He shall gnash with his teeth, and melt away. The desire of the wicked shall perish. Create in

**me a clean heart and renew a right spirit within me."
(Psalms 51:10).**

Princeton wanted his heart fixed (spiritually)!!! He wanted his heart healed. He knew God would give him a new heart and take away his stony (sick) heart. He had not been afraid of evil tidings (bad news about his heart). He had trusted in God.

Princeton knew his heart needed an overhaul. He would settle for nothing less than a new heart, a perfect heart, a clean heart, a fixed heart, a merry heart, a pure heart, a wise and understanding heart, and a whole heart, so he could "love God with his whole heart."

And he had realized that Christ had died on the cross to take away his imperfect heart only to give him a perfect heart void of any impurities and sin. Princeton believed with all his heart that what satan had intended for his bad, God had made it good." "All things work together for good to them who love the Lord, who are the called unto his purpose" (Romans 8:28).

Had Princeton not gotten a negative report on the condition of his heart, he would never have sought or meditated daily upon the heart of Christ or the heart of God!!! Now, like the lady who was healed of the issue of blood, Princeton knew within himself that he was healed in his heart of every heart condition.

Previously, he was one of those men whose heart had [almost] failed him due to fear (Luke 21:26). "Never again," said Princeton, "will I allow my heart to be overwhelmed by fear." "Perfect Love casteth out fear, for fear hath torment (1 John 4:18) and heart problems would no longer torment Princeton. He had a new, cheerful and merry heart. Princeton was full of joy!!!

With respect to Princeton's diagnosis of stomach cancer, he came to realize the real reason he had contracted sickness in that part of his body. Due to the intensive and extensive readings, Princeton came to the knowledge that satan only attacks the part of the body that God anointed.

That is why Princeton danced for joy when Miracle had read these words to him out loud: "He that believeth on me, as the Scriptures hath said, out of his belly shall flow rivers of living water. (But this spake He of the Spirit, which they that believe on Him should receive; for the Holy Ghost was not yet given; because that Jesus was not yet glorified (John 7:38,39).

The Word, in its entirety that Miracle had read to him day after day, was pouring out of Princeton like water. "Was God calling him into the ministry to preach the Gospel? Was God calling him away from the earthly throne that his mom and dad treasured above any material possession?" thought Princeton.

Princeton had focused on Jonah, and how had been in the belly for three days and nights, and how Jonah had prayed to God out of the fish's belly (Jonah 1:17; 2:1). Princeton enjoyed the outcome of Jonah's dilemma, "And the Lord spake unto the fish, and it vomited out Jonah upon the dry land (Jonah 2:10).

That was the turning point when Princeton knew with every fiber of his being that he had been healed of stomach cancer. He had vomited several months ago. Not only had God spoken to his stomach cancer personally as a result of the daily readings with Miracle, he himself had learned to speak to the mountain so it would be moved (Matthew 21:21).

And lastly, Miracle had read one last Scripture concerning his belly: Revelation 10:8-11 which says, "and the voice which I heard from Heaven spake unto me again, and said, Go and take the little book which is open in the hand of the angel which standeth upon the sea, and upon the earth.

And I went unto the angel, and said unto him, give me this little book. And he said unto me, Take it, and eat it up, and it shall make thy belly bitter, but it shall be in thy mouth sweet as honey. And I took the little book out of the angel's hand, and ate it up, and it was in my mouth sweet as honey; and as soon as I had eaten it, my belly was bitter. And he said unto me, thou must prophesy again before many peoples, and nations, and tongues, and kings."

Princeton, with Miracle's help, had taken the Scriptures, and read them so many times until both he and Miracle were full of Perfect Healing and Perfect Health— so much so until it would be impossible for any sickness or disease that had attached itself to any part of their human body to stay.

Diabetes had been another story. Most people think that once you have diabetes, there is no cure for the disease except medication and proper diet. Princeton would prove them all wrong. He just believed there was a cure for every illness known to man.

Princeton went deep inside himself to figure out why diabetes had become a stronghold in his life. Had the sweetness gone out of his life? Did he just need to believe more convincingly that *life is sweet!!!*

Princeton did not believe that his diabetes had been genetic simply because one or more of his relatives—immediate or extended—may be diabetics. To date, no one in his family was a diabetic. Of that he was certain. But, even if they were, no one had the right to imply that he was predisposed to diabetes.

Jesus Christ, God's Son, had died on the cross over two thousand years ago to take away his diabetes, and to leave in its stead Permanent Perfect Healing and Perfect Health. If Jesus had taken away his diabetes on that cross two thousand years ago, and that diabetes had been nailed to the cross with Christ, and then buried as well with Christ in the tomb, not to rise with Christ on the Third Day, then why should Princeton insult Christ's Atonement on the cross by still carrying diabetes in his body?

The way Princeton read into the Gospel message, it was clear that God had never intended for anyone on the earth to live in any physical state other than Perfect Health. Therefore, Princeton could only conclude that Christ's death on the cross ensured that he would never have to live with any illness such as diabetes, now or anytime in the future.

The Word of God (Scriptures) and the Blood of the Lamb would cure his diabetes. No matter what medical science had to say, "This sickness (diabetes) was not unto death, but for the Glory of God, that the Son of God might be glorified thereby" (John 11:4).

Though diabetes had been the most difficult of his three illnesses to rid himself of once and for all, Princeton was not to be denied. He had read in Habakkah 2:1-3 these words: "I will stand upon my watch, and set me upon the tower, and I will watch to see what He will say unto me, and what I shall answer when I am reproved. And the Lord answered me, and said, write the vision, and make it plain upon tables, that he may run that readeth it. For the vision is yet for an appointed time, but at the end it shall speak, and not lie, though it tarry, wait for it, because it will surely come; it will not tarry."

Ever since the diagnosis one year ago, Princeton had held on to the words found in Psalms 37:10: "For yet a little while, and the wicked shall not be. Yea, thou shalt diligently consider his place, and it shall not be," as well as the words found in ( ): "My heart is inditing a good matter" (Psalms 45:1).

Princeton had held on to the vision of going to medical doctors and hearing the words, "Who told you that you were a diabetic? There is no trace of diabetes anywhere in your body!!!"

To put the icing on the cake, Princeton envisioned the medical doctor who gave him the initial diagnosis being so speculative and curious about how he had gotten cured from diabetes until he had personally ordered multiple tests to confirm the perfect healing.

Princeton's A1C was below 6.5. His blood sugar was normal two hours after each meal. He had been taken to the Veteran's Hospital for one week, ad they had spent every minute poking and prodding Princeton for specimens and blood, and other tests he did not know by name.

Two hours after breakfast, lunch, and dinner the lab technicians were knocking at his hospital door for "more blood." Each time, the results came back the same. "There is no more diabetes. Now, every diabetic and everyone associated with the Diabetic Association were on hand to uncover how Princeton was healed of diabetes.

For that matter just about everybody was on hand to discuss Princeton's overall health after it had upgraded from dismal to Perfect. What had he done to get healed? Would his techniques work for anyone else or everyone else with any terminal illness?

"What most people do not think about," said Princeton, "is that no one was born to live forever here on planet earth once Adam and Eve committed the first sin *way back when!!!* So, God literally could not and should not have to take the blame for Adam and Eve's blunder."

God had created Adam and Eve in a State of Perfect Health that was to last for eternity. Perfect Health for the entire human race had always been and would always be God's Perfect Will. It had been Lucifer, now known as satan, who is the cause of all sin, suffering, and atrocities we experience today.

Satan will fortunately be brought to justice once and for all once he is cast into the lake of fire, never to deceive or hurt anyone else ever again. Then everyone will live happily ever after in the New Heaven and the New Earth. Princeton therefore felt justified when he said, "It was just not my time to go or to "kick the bucket yet!!! God had other plans for me."

Up to this point, no one had known Princeton was anything but a picture of Perfect Health, not even the king and queen, and especially not even Miracle Faith Love, which had some sneaking suspicions that anything might be wrong or out of the ordinary.

For Princeton, timing was everything!!! Nothing could stand in the way or jeopardize Princeton's highly-spirited determination to be read back into Perfect Health!!!

As for Princeton, the extensive and intensive daily Readings by Miracle, the fastings, the prayers, the thanksgivings, the praises, and the worship services, not to mention the Biblical meditation and move to Hawaii—all had lent a hand in Princeton's totally Perfect Health status.

Princeton could not have asked for anything more except perhaps for Miracle Faith Love's hand in marriage. Next to God and Christ, Miracle was the greatest miracle of all!!!

As for Miracle Faith Love, she needed a miracle of her own. Until the night she had fallen apart and literally burst into tears in Princeton's presence as she was reading, she never knew she needed healing.

The incest had left its mark on Miracle. She had gone so deep within herself that no one would ever find her. That was why she had gone into Reading in the first place. With a graduate degree in Reading, Miracle could use that as her chosen vehicle of choice to escape, lose herself, and act as if she did not exist on the planet.

Miracle had found her own healing. She had healed the incest that she had buried away since childhood. She had done it through the process of reading daily to Princeton. What an irony!!! Princeton had never really came straight out and said anything to her concerning his health issues, but during the one Reading Assignment of her lifetime she had literally read herself straight into her own healing.

Miracle's career in Reading had allowed her to transport herself to anywhere she wanted to go. Reading, for Miracle, was her Miracle, her Faith, and her love. Her readings had sustained her, and had given her hope when others would never have survived such a tragedy. She was stronger than she knew. She would never be the same!!!

Of course, Miracle now knew that such a coping mechanism had only slowed down her own healing process and had kept her stuck in the aftermath of the incest. What she did not know is that denying the fact that the incest had actually happened was her body's way of keeping her safe until it was safe to come out of her isolated existence called life.

Miracle had been hiding herself in her work at The Reading Agency unconsciously, thus cutting herself off from the world, and the healing that was 100% inevitable.

Miracle loved Reading beyond words. She was born to read!!! She had no earthly idea that all the Scriptures she had read to Princeton day after day for the past several months was literally reading her like a book.

That was why Miracle had cried at Princeton's mansion for the first time since the incest had taken place. She had to give such an atrocity a name and put a face to it to see it for all it was worth, but she had not realized such a revelation at the time of her outburst.

Miracle had hated herself for crying openly in front of Princeton. She prided herself in only crying at funerals, which she made a point not to go to unless it was absolutely imperative—meaning someone very close to her.

Miracle had been fighting to stay in control of the very life that she felt the incest stole from her. Of course, no one else would notice that her life was out of order, but she was somewhat, if not greatly overwhelmed, in carrying such a heavy burden no one would not really understand unless they had experienced the same incestuous tragedy!

Miracle had no idea that God had decided it was time for her to experience a miraculous healing of her own. God needed for Miracle to tear down the walls she had built around herself.

Somehow, through the Readings, Miracle had "let Princeton in," which she never did for anyone for any reason. Before coming to Hawaii, Miracle had never dwelt too long on the thought of marriage, though she felt lonely at times. She felt like Humpty Dumpty who could not be put together again by anyone.

During her Readings of the Healing Scriptures, Miracle stumbled upon these two Scriptures: "For thus saith the Lord of Hosts; yet once, it is a little while, and I will shake the heavens, and the earth, and the sea, and the dry land, and I will shake all nations, and the desire of all nations shall come, and I will fill this house with Glory, saith the Lord of Hosts. The silver is mine, and the gold is mine, saith the Lord of Hosts. The Glory of this latter house shall be greater than the former, saith the Lord of Hosts, and in this place will I give peace, saith the Lord of Hosts" (Haggai 2:6-9).

"Behold, at that time, I will undo all that afflict thee. I will save them that halteth. I will gather them that was driven out, and I will get her praise in every land where thou was put to shame" (Zephaniah 3:19).

From the time of Reading these prophetic words that could only come from God Himself, Miracle would never see life the same way again. Princeton had thought to himself on many occasions of how Miracle's Readings had brought him miraculously back to life.

Miracle was getting her life back as well!!! She was about to experience Reading on a whole new spectrum. Her love for Reading was about to take on a new direction of its own in ways most people she knew had never taken the time to consider!

Chapter Ten

The Reading Proposal

Miracle very seldom went out on dates. She was not the type. With her glasses, and the way she wore her hair up, as well as the way she wore her lab coat, one might at first glance, think Miracle was a scientist conducting an experiment in a science or biology lab.

Wearing this white lab coat made Miracle feel safe and protected from the outside world and all negative influences. It had never dawned on Miracle that she had an obsessive need to be surrounded by the color white.

In fact, in Princeton, New Jersey, one could easily notice the white décor of many of her quintessential rooms. Miracle loved white. She had been ecstatic when upon her being hired by Princeton to work at The Reading Agency, he had informed her that it was perfectly okay if she had a professional interior decorator to paint her office walls white and furnish it with white chairs, carpeting, and accessories. Only her office desk was rich, mahogany brown.

As homely as Miracle thought she looked, sometimes on purpose, she could hardly believe her luck when she had accidently read Princeton's Reading (Marriage) Proposal last evening after surprisingly enjoying his company at the luau on the other side of the beautiful Hawaiian island. All Miracle could think about was how last night's Reading Proposal had transpired.

Despite not liking the view of the islander's roasting a pig large enough to feed an army, Miracle had thoroughly enjoyed the ham, pineapple, as well as the lively, upbeat music. She cannot remember when she had had so much fun—laughing and dancing. She had spent so much time in her Readings she had little time for anyone else or anything else. She wanted it that way!!!

The whole night, Miracle had wondered why Princeton had stolen glances at her when he did not think she was looking. Of course, as usual, she brushed such a question aside once Princeton and she took a stroll down the now deserted beach.

Millions of stars were shining brightly, and the feel of the ocean's water against her bare heels and ankles as the tide came in was nothing short of sheer, absolute exhilaration—one emotion she did not allow herself to feel unless she was engaged in Reading. Neither Princeton nor Miracle wanted the night to end. So they just continued to walk down the beach, and enjoyed each other's silent presence.

Princeton Miles III was a Prince after all, and he would use that position to coax Miracle into reading several documents he deliberately left on his coffee table in his living room—the one room of the house where Miracle Felt safe.

"Miracle, I know it is late. It is way past 2:00 a.m., but do you mind taking a look at one of the Scriptures I typed out for you to read during our next Reading Session? Tell me what you think. Give me that personal spin that only you can give!!! Read every single word out loud." (Princeton had deliberately put the Reading Proposal on the bottom of the stack he would hand her when the time came).

Just like clockwork, Miracle did read out loud every single word of the Scripture Princeton gave her, not to mention the other Readings as well. When she got to the very last page, she just continued reading automatically: "Miracle, you are an angel, and since coming to Hawaii, I have fallen deeply in love with you. You are the love of my life!!! Say that you will marry me and abide with me forever, until "death do us part!!!""

As she started to read the Reading Proposal, half way through it, Princeton got down on one knee, pulling out of his pocket a solid gold jewelry box. Opening the box to look inside, Princeton pulled out a 40-Karat diamond engagement ring. The yellow gold band itself was so transparent, Miracle could see her reflection in it.

The exceptional sparkle of the larger than life diamond was phenomenal. It was nothing short of what a king would buy for his queen. In fact, the ring had belonged to his mother, the queen, which had been an heirloom that had passed down to her from her very own mother. She had wished that such a brilliant ring would be presented to his future bride.

Miracle expected nothing less from Princeton's selection of a ring, given his royal status, but she was not a financial slouch by anyone's standards. Reading and meditating on these words in Joshua 1:8 daily had brought Miracle into Infinite Wealth.

"But this book of the law shall not depart out of thy mouth, but thou shalt meditate therein day and night that thou mayest observe to do according to all that is written therein. Then thou shalt make thy way prosperous and then thou shalt have good success."

Miracle had literally read her way into Great Substance. She had read the story in 1 Kings 3 of how King Solomon had become the richest King in the world. No king would match that wealth. Yet Jesus had said, "A greater than Solomon [Jesus] is here."

Miracle was filthy rich and fabulously wealthy. That was why she had not been so taken back by Princeton's position as a prince, as was every female in Princeton, New Jersey or in any location in the world where Princeton found himself.

Miracle did not feel the need to flaunt her wealth. She just loved to read, and she lived to read—for herself—to herself—and to others. Reading was her life, and Princeton Miles III was asking her to become a part of his life as Mrs. Princeton Miles III.

How would her life change—as Princeton's wife, and as his queen? She had no desire to be a princess, let alone a queen. What would the queen think of her? Would his mother think of her as a "gold-digger?"

Miracle thought of all the times she had spent at The Reading Agency devising Reading Curricula for each one of her Readees. She had thought of Princeton as a fascinating man, but she never thought of him "like that" or in any other kind of romantic way, let alone as her husband!!!

She had felt, however, a certain chemistry developing between the two of them here on Hawaiian soil—a chemistry she had tried to push aside for the sake of business etiquette and professionalism.

Miracle had first felt that chemistry at Princeton's mansion the night she sobbed uncontrollably. But, they both believed in "waiting for the wedding night." They both were virgins and they had too much respect for one another to go against such a belief.

Yet, so many times, Miracle had wanted to reach out to Princeton—to embrace him for the simple fact that they both needed a long, overdue hug. As husband and wife, she could hug Princeton forever. But, for right now, she and her future husband had a wedding to plan!!!

Chapter Eleven

The Reading Ability

Miracle Faith Love was to Princeton Miles III everything that his mother was not. He knew the moment Miracle walked into The Reading Agency that she would not think twice or feel put out about Reading to him whatever his heart desired. She was not the type of woman who would leave him hanging to pursue a measly royal throne. She was not only a woman of Great Means and Great Substance, she was a woman of Great Balance.

Princeton was a mama's boy at heart, though the queen had been much too busy in her royal duties to take the time to read to him nightly as he had so desperately craved to be read to the way a thirsty person might need water.

Princeton would never marry a female who was not passionate about Reading!!! "Better than anyone at The Reading Agency, Miracle understood that Reading was a passport to the world and to the future!!! Just one word read out loud could usher the most adventurous boy to anywhere in the world," thought Princeton.

By the time Miracle finished reading, you could close your eyes and feel as though you could travel to any remote part of the globe that your heart desired. Miracle had the Reading Ability to take the Readee to any destination— past, present, or future.

"Right now," Princeton thought, "I must be in Heaven. My future wife-to-be is an angel." He would check in with God momentarily to verify if an angel was missing in Heaven!!!

There was also another side to Miracle that caught Princeton off guard—and he was never caught off guard by anything or anyone, expect perhaps for his domineering mother. Miracle had the insight to read into any situation, and she had read his family—his royal family like a book. She had come up with a Perfect Solution to his predicament of the possibility of turning his back on the throne as a future king to live a normal life.

Miracle had read of how some not so wealthy individuals engage in what she called the "either/or mentality," where you can have one thing, but not the two. For example, "I would rather be healthy than wealthy!!!" Or, "I may need to be healthy, but I want to be wealthy instead!!!"

None of these well-meaning individuals would ever think, "I can be healthy <u>and </u>wealthy!!!" "I can have plenty of money and still be happy and healthy!!!" Or, I can marry for love <u>and</u> money, rather than having to choose between the love or the money."

Miracle suggested to Princeton the idea of maintaining his privacy and normalcy while at the same time keeping his mother happy by not relinquishing the throne. Not that she would be running down the aisle just to be "the future queen." Miracle was used to living alone, being on her own, being independent and not needing anyone.

Being through what she had been through, Miracle had learned to see life from more than one point of view. She would appeal to the heart of the queen personally and privately so she herself could make the necessary transition into not just the royal family with its royal duties, but into a family in general. Miracle would see to it that the king and queen's wishes for their son would be realized in ways none of them had anticipated.

Miracle maintained that "Princeton could have it all"—love, marriage, children (lots of children), a career beyond the throne, as well as his position on the throne. "After all," said Miracle, the queen loves her son more than anyone, including Princeton, would ever know!!!"

Surely, once the queen grasped the idea that her son would not go missing in action (MIA) if she stepped aside and gave him a little more personal space and freedom to live his own life, that he would only make an even greater and happier king when the time came.

Meanwhile, Princeton was anticipating giving his beloved wife-to-be the fairytale wedding every young girl dreams about—or should dream about. For the rest of his life, Princeton Miles III would make his wife feel like the royalty she had made him feel every time she stepped into his physical presence. His Miracle would never go to bed or sleep each night without feeling like a princess or queen!!! He would see to it personally!!!

Princeton would go out of his way to bestow all his earthly goods and wealth, not to mention undying love, upon his wife daily. She would have the best this Universe could offer. She would not want for anything!!! He would never leave her side for one instant, for any reason. He was hers to hold henceforth and forevermore!!!

Chapter Twelve

The Royal Wedding

Just as Princess Diana walked down the aisle to her husband, Prince Charles, so did Miracle Faith Love walk down the aisle to her beloved Princeton. The massive cathedral could barely hold the more than 5,000 invited guests who were smiling profusely at Miracle as she and Princeton's father, the king, slowly made their way down the aisle to the altar.

In attendance were the Heads of State of every foreign country in the world, as well as every First Lady, every Prime Minister, and the President of the United States and his First Lady. This was Miracle's day and they all were here for her—to celebrate such a momentous and memorable occasion!!!

Miracle had grown up in the state of Maine and she had moved to Princeton, New Jersey when Princeton offered her the Reading Position seven years ago. She had willingly traveled to Hawaii for a one-year stay when Princeton needed her to read to him—for reasons she had not known about. However, she elected not to marry her Prince Charming in the United States.

She had been one of the many people who had watched the televised royal wedding of Princess Diana and Prince Charles. She was only a small girl at the time, but even at such a tender, young age, she had wanted to feel like royalty on her wedding day.

Miracle vowed to marry in one of the largest cathedrals in London, England. And today, she was getting married at St. Paul's Cathedral, the second largest cathedral building in the United Kingdom after the Liverpool Cathedral— the same cathedral in which Princess Dianna and Prince Charles were married.

Britain had rolled out the red carpet for Miracle as they welcomed her into their homeland. The attendants had no problem holding the long train of Miracle Faith Love that extended from the altar itself to the entrance of the cathedral.

Just as "Princess Diana and Prince Charles had emerged as husband and wife in 1981 from the West Porch, approached from Ludgate, (the main entrance to the cathedral, so did Miracle Faith Love embark upon that same entrance into St. Paul's Cathedral to make her way to the high altar to exchange marriage vows with her knight in shining armor.

"Ooh's" and "aah's" had been gasped as Princeton and his best man, Prince Bouvier France II entered the cathedral from its side door. Princeton looked charming and dashing in his formal Air Force Military Attire. Later, as prince, he would change into his royal apparel that was fit for a king!!!

The queen looked absolutely dazzling and stunning in her most elegant evening gown. Atop her immaculately looking hair graced the crown jewel itself with jewelry that was nothing short of Heaven.

Just last evening, the queen was so happy about her son's marriage to Miracle, she deliberately placed that same crown upon Miracle's head, as a sign and token of her undying affection for the happy couple. She wanted her new daughter in law to feel like a queen on the most special day of her life—especially since Miracle had let her in on her incestuous past.

Princeton and his dad cried. They had just witnessed the greatest miracle of all—the queen did not take a liking to "just anyone." To extend her beloved crown to Miracle on the eve of the wedding ceremony—their ceremony— meant everything to Princeton. Miracle was now officially a part of the royal family, and the best was yet to come!!!

Everyone in the larger—than life cathedral broke out in uninterrupted, thunderous applause when they heard the Bishop say, "I now pronounce you husband and wife. I now present to the congregation for the first time in Holy Matrimony Mr. and Mrs. Princeton Miles III—Your Highness, Prince Princeton Miles III and Princess Miracle Faith Love."

Princeton had outdone himself in asking the Bishop to deliberately announce the newly wedded couple in two unique ways—first as husband and wife, without royalty status (Princeton's idea of normalcy), and secondly as royalty—to make his wife feel like a princess on her wedding day.

As long as she lived, Miracle would never forget this day—a day that had more than made up for all other days of Miracle's life—especially unwanted sexual molestation.

For added emphasis, both Princeton and Miracle walked in a dignified, somber manner before the king and queen, and bowed. Everyone's healing was now complete!!! This royal wedding was just what Christ, the Great Physician, had ordered. Christ, Himself, in all His Glory, Splendor, and Majesty, had made his Kingly Presence felt in the cathedral amongst everyone in attendance. The throne was still intact!!! And so was God's and the Lamb of God's!!!

For one brief moment, not a single person in the cathedral moved for what seemed like an eternity!!! The queen broke the hushed silence by standing up, stepping away from her beloved throne inside the cathedral, to embrace first her new daughter in law, then her only beloved Princeton. The moment the queen hugged Miracle, in front of all the guests, Miracle burst out in happy tears. This had been a long time coming!!!

Miracle held on to her new mother in law for the very first time and she did not—could not—let go right away. The queen knew—the queen understood—the queen cared—just as Miracle had suspected along.

The queen realized what this day of all days meant to a young girl who had survived incest—to a young girl who never believed a wedding day would happen for her. "My throne, my door, my home, and my heart are always open to you, my daughter," whispered the queen to Miracle. "You are royalty." "You are a royal priesthood and a chosen generation (1 Peter 2:9).

Princeton was a strong man. He had survived cancer, diabetes, and heart problems without traditional medicine, but he almost collapsed at his mother's embrace—the first, but most definitely not the last!!!

The king stepped down from the throne upon which he had so graciously sat to embrace his son for the very first time. "Son, I have been a big fool, not spending enough time with you the way I wanted to. I have a lot of catching up to do in the hugging department. Do you think you can give your "ole man" a hug?"

By this time, no one really felt lie going to the huge wedding reception the royal family and the royal couple had planned together. They just wanted to "hang out." But, for Miracle's sake, they all went through the motions of enjoying the extravagant buffet that was fit for the wealthiest king and queen.

Later, much later this evening, Prince Princeton Miles III and Princess Miracle Faith Love would be flying by the royal plane, first to the Virgin Islands for a month (a spot deliberately chosen by Miracle to expedite her total deliverance and never-expected healing to purposely consummate the marriage Miracle never thought would happen) on her honeymoon, and then thereafter they would fly back to Hawaii to tie up some much-needed loose ends with respect to Princeton's status as future king.

Epilogue

Princeton and Miracle honeymooned in the Virgin Islands for two months, enjoying one another, in addition to exploring the sites extensively and intently before traveling back to Hawaii. Once married, Miracle had felt comfortable moving into Princeton's mansion as husband and wife. Before, with the exception of Princeton's guided tour when she first went to Hawaii, Miracle had never stepped foot in any of the rooms other than the living room. Princeton had always been the Perfect gentleman!!!

Now, they had to rethink their living arrangements and estates. Miracle Faith Love was expecting twin boys on October 13, 2013. Princeton, at one time had wanted to relinquish his throne and move to Hawaii—once and for all. It had been in the state of Hawaii where Miracle had read him back to life and Perfect Health!!!

Things were different now—much different! Miracle was determined that her twin boys—Ethan Allen and Evan Allen—would not grow up without their grandparents, the king and queen, in the way Princeton had grown up without his parents. Miracle would see to that personally.

The honeymoon had been so Perfect. Both Princeton and Miracle had time to really think about their future as husband and wife, as prince and princess, as the future king and queen, and as proud parents to be.

Everyone had agreed that Princeton would attend Seminary School Online as he pursued a Bachelor's Degree in Biblical Studies, a Master's in Ministry, and a Doctorate in Divinity. God was calling him into the ministry with a specialty in a healing, thanksgiving, praise and worship ministry.

His parents had saturated every waking moment of his young life preparing him for an earthly throne. Since his Readings in Hawaii with Miracle, he had come to know personally the Lord of Lords and King of Kings—the Christ who would one day sit on the seat of His Father David, as head of the Kingdom of God in the New Heaven and the New Earth!!!

All Babylon systems of government (all rulership other than Christ) will be put down. "The kingdoms of this world have become the kingdoms of our Lord and of His Christ" (Revelation 11:15) Christ shall reign upon the earth.

His two boys would be taught both systems of the government—the American Government, as well as Christ's Government, so they would always know to choose Christ's Rule and Lordship over any earthly political system, even if it were the king and queen's throne.

His boys would come to know the power of thanksgiving, praise, and worship, just as he had when Miracle read him back to Perfect Health. More than a million "Thank you's" had gotten him the victory over terminal illness. Such a feat was only the tip of the iceberg, to say the least. His two sons would surpass his own accomplishments in the thanksgiving, praise and worship department.

Princeton's favorite Scriptures—Acts 13:2 and Luke 2:36-37 reads thusly: "As they ministered to the Lord and fasted, the Holy Ghost said, Separate me Barnabus and Saul for the work whereunto I have called them." "And there was one Anna, a prophetess, the daughter of Phanuel, of the tribe of Aser; she was of a great age, and had lived with a husband seven years from her virginity; and she was a widow of about fourscore and four years, <u>which departed not from the temple, but served God with fastings and prayers night and day</u>."

Also, Princeton had come to love the following Scriptures as well: "I exhort therefore that, first of all, supplications, prayers, intercessions, and giving of thanks, be made for all men: for kings, and for all that are in authority; that we may lead a quiet and peaceable life in al godliness and honesty" (1 Timothy 2:1-2).

"Is any among you afflicted? Let him pray. Is any merry? Let him sing psalms. Is any sick among you? Let him call for the elders of the church; and let them pray over him, anointing him with oil in the name of the Lord. And the prayer of faith shall save the sick, and the Lord shall raise him up; and if he has committed sins, they shall be forgiven him. Confess your faults one to another, that ye may be healed. The effectual payers of a righteous man availeth much" (James 5:13-16).

Princeton's boys would learn to minister to God and for those on the throne, as well as for anyone who was in authority upon the earth. No greater thing they could do than to offer themselves to God as a Minister of Intercession in the ministry of intercession.

That was the highest form of government—all kings should bow down to the Lord of lords. "Wherefore God also hath highly exalted Him, and given Him a name which is above every name. That at the name of Jesus every knee should bow, of things in Heaven, and things in earth, and things under the earth; and that every tongue should confess that Jesus Christ is Lord to the Glory of God the Father" (Philippians 2:9).

As for Miracle, she would enroll in the same Seminary School Online to pursue an accredited Bachelor's Degree in Biblical Studies, a Master's in Christian Education, and a Doctorate in Divinity to complement her former degrees.

She wanted to combine the subject of Reading, Christian Education Techniques and Advanced Worship to devise a Christian Education Curriculum that she could use throughout her pregnancy and after such a blessed childbirth.

Princeton and Miracle, together, would use such curricula during their family devotions, before and after their boys were born, to give them a Spiritual Headstart in life. They wanted to devise a prenatal Bible Curriculum where their boys would learn from the womb how to say, "Thank you God!!!" "Thank you Lord!!!" "Thank you Jesus!!!" "Thank you Holy Spirit!!!" "Thank you Holy Ghost!!!" And "Thank you Jehovah!!!" Billions of times a day. His twin boys would learn at a very early age how to say "Thank you" in over 400 languages!!!

As prenatals, their two sons would be formally introduced to the God who created them, and the Christ who died for them so they could have Eternal Life. Their two boys—Ethan and Evan would bow the knee to Jehovah and Christ, and not to Baal or satan in false worship.

In conclusion, Princeton, Miracle, their two twin boys, and the king and queen would live happily ever after. Everyone had a blast taking turns Reading bed time stories, the Bible, and other books to the boys before and after they were born.

Princeton and Miracle kept their mansion in Hawaii and visited there often during the winter months, but they elected to live in a mansion near the king and queen's palace in Princeton, New Jersey. What man or woman in his or her right mind would walk away from a Billion hugs a day from the king and queen?

Princeton and Miracle never forgot the Power of Reading. For them, Reading had opened up miracles, faith, and love that surpassed their own understanding.

As for the rest of the world and medical science, they are still trying to figure out exactly what exactly led to Princeton's mysterious and baffling Perfect Healing.

Was it just the Readings with Miracle Faith Love? Was it just the thanksgiving? Was it just the Praise? Was it just the worship? Was it just the fastings? Was it just a miracle? Was it just faith? Was it just love? Was it some of the above, all of the above, or none of the above?

No one knows for sure, but there was one thing Princeton and Miracle did know without a doubt. Never underestimate the Great Physician, Christ, the Infallible Word of God, or The Reading Specialist, who is now thinking about taking The Reading Agency and her husband's Praise and Worship Center and His Ministry of Intercession world-wide.